THE
ROOMMATE

INTERNATIONAL BESTSELLING AUTHOR
TK LAWYER

1

Nya

Carter threw open the door, took one long look at me, and then furrowed his eyebrows with concern. He lowered his tone of voice to a soothing murmur.

"Oh no… Come here, baby girl."

I walked into his open arms and leaned my head into his broad, nude, sexy-as-hell-bronzed chest. Then, slowly, I exhaled, melting my upper body into his with a soft smile. My forehead encountered scratchy, chin stubble as he lowered his handsome face to mine. His arms swept me into the warmest, tightest hug. I allowed my body to collapse into a state of sweet bliss for the first time that day.

Carter slammed the door behind us, concern, etching deep frown lines across his forehead. "I'm sorry, Nya. He was a jackass. He didn't deserve you."

I closed my eyes, my heart grateful for this peaceful moment. His nimble fingers threaded easily through my long, dark brown hair. A swirling sensation started low in my gut and then streamed pleasure through me, zipping sensuously straight to my head, clouding it in a mind-blowing sensorial fog. Carter held me still while I inhaled, taking one long whiff of his manly musk. *My god. How I needed him right now*. My knees weakened. I leaned into him as my jaw loosened and almost spilled the secret I held deep within me.

Losing myself in the safety and security of my best friend, I was more than ready to forget what happened earlier today and get on with the rest of the night.

His strong arms suddenly dropped to his sides. A sharp, cold sensation enveloped me. Carter stepped away from me as if we hadn't just had a beautiful moment of bliss and walked toward the kitchen. "You hungry?" he called out.

I ignored the sadness that spiraled through me, threatening to tear me down.

"Sure am." I rushed toward him, ready to continue what we started despite my stomach entertaining other available pleasures. I hadn't eaten since the incident, but I was not hungry for food. Grabbing ahold of his hand, I stared into his perfect brown irises, captivated by the sparkling flecks I found there. I stared at his full lips. Recalled moments in time with Carter that made me happy. I was ready to re-enact any of those moments.

I tugged at his arm, giving him a flirty smile at the same time as I motioned him toward his bedroom.

He smirked. "Oh, I see… Are you sure you don't want to eat first? It will give you energy."

I winked. "You think I can't keep up?" I tugged harder at his wrist, hoping he would get the message. "Oh no. I'm good. I just need you."

"Well then..." He gave me a wicked smile at first before he pulled me further into the kitchen and shoved my back gently against a counter. He cornered me with his broad, smoking-hot chest. "Let me take your mind off of Eddie."

He lowered his head, matching his lips to mine, and gave me the sweetest kiss. His fingers worked while his lips entertained me, lifting my shirt, slightly teasing the edge of my leggings. He strummed his thumbs back and forth in a dizzying motion across my waist.

I planted kisses across his chest, nibbling at his darkened nipples, and then threw my head back and sighed. "Oh Carter… Don't play with me."

He gave me a wide, toothy grin seconds before he nuzzled my neck. "But it's so much fun, Nya."

Plunging his fingers beneath the stretchy fabric, he slowly rolled it down, at the same time leaning toward me and planting passionate kisses down my chest. Swirls of pleasure sprang up from the sensitive, sweet spot between my legs. He inched closer toward his destination while my breath turned into gasps for life-sustaining oxygen.

My excitement heightened. I watched him, admiring the smoothness of his moves seconds before he lowered himself to kneel, kissing his way down my panty and across my left thigh. My leggings were now pooled around my ankles. I rolled my head in a dizzying slow motion while I panted heavily, waiting on the edge of my seat in anticipation of what was yet to come. Carter was *so*—good. So very, very *good*.

He gave me that sexy "I got you" grin that silently reassured me that he would take care of me and that everything would be all right.

His fingers explored the outside of my panty and then slipped gently beneath the flimsy material. He teased me mercilessly with lazy, mind-numbing circles across my folds, delving deeper and deeper with every sensual swirl of his capable fingers. *My lord. This man was going to be the death of me.* I threw my head back and whimpered while my heartbeat galloped like a prized racehorse toward the finish line. My pussy and my breasts arched toward him, aching and throbbing with longing and unfulfilled desire. I needed him *bad*. Only Carter could fulfill my great need.

My brain retorted. *Damn. Had it been that long?*

Possibly. Eddie was never around, it seemed. Since I started dating him, I didn't dare ask Carter to take care of my needs when Eddie wasn't.

Despite my roommate's nasty reputation as a player and a womanizer, I was unlike him. I was a one guy, type of girl. Once I was with a man, I was *with* him. I didn't play around. I didn't look for anyone else. Yet now that Eddie and I were done... My possibilities seemed open and endless.

Carter groaned as he rubbed his hands all over my bare bottom, giving each butt cheek a gentle squeeze. He came up for air. "Damn Nya. I love how wet you get for me. I've only just begun."

"God, Carter, you are sooo good. Please don't make me wait any longer for you. Please... I've had a shitty day. I just want release."

He quirked his head up. "Oh. Is that all I am to you? A sex toy?" He teased me with a wink.

"Please, no. You know you are so much more to me than that."

I looked into his eyes. I could have sworn I saw something resembling awe and admiration floating in there. But nah—that wasn't Carter at all. He liked women. They were useful to him when he needed something for a night or two. He never stayed with any of them for long. The corners of his mouth curled up into a sweet smile. "As are you—my beautiful best friend."

His words hit me hard like a cold, wet towel slapped across my over-heated face.

There it was. The definition of our relationship. *Friends*. Now friends with benefits.

We became friends back in high school. Back then, he was the nerd that was into tech and gadgets while I was the bookworm, my nose always buried in the next novel. After high school, we decided to move in together. We had been roommates for almost one year before we started exploring a different side of our friendship.

I had to be honest. There were days I wished for more. Still, I can't say I regret crossing over the barrier from the traditional role of friendship. When I needed him, he was there for me. When he needed me, I was there for him. The only problem was he didn't seem to need me as much as I needed him.

He slipped his index finger beneath my panty and followed it with another. His fingers teased the edges of my pussy, touching, groping, and playing with me until I was ready to scream or beg for him to make me come. Or both.

My heavy panting quickly turned into bursts of exhales and inhales as Carter toyed with me. He swept his glorious fingers over my clit and then plunged two of them into my wet pussy, scissoring in and out at a rapid pace that threatened to stop the life-giving oxygen streaming in and out of my starved lungs. I licked my lips and gyrated my hips to his sensual rhythm. "Carter, please…"

His husky tone of voice caressed my eardrums. "Yes, Nya. What do you want?"

My voice stuttered as I struggled to speak. "You babe. You. Now."

He tugged at my panty, tearing at it until it gave way, rolling the remnants all the way down until it joined the top of my leggings.

He paused, staring at my nakedness, speechless and with an innocent look of pure fascination in his eyes that caused the start of tears to form in my own. "Beautiful."

I blinked several times, determined not to cry at this intimate moment. "Damn, Carter, you're so impatient. Now I have to buy new underwear," I teased, making light of the moment while also making a mental note to purchase another pair of black lace thongs since he tore up the one I had been wearing. Carter always liked the color black across my creamy complexion. I always obliged him, buying his preference so I could get more of him- anytime

I wanted. It was a sneaky ploy, but it mostly worked to my benefit.

He winked. "I'll help you pick out some if you'd like."

I snorted. "No, I can choose my own. Thanks." I stopped myself from saying more, the urge to spew out what I thought about his casual dating lifestyle clawing at my insides. Carter had a right to date who he wanted. He had a right to pursue his own happiness. He could buy underwear for those chicks if he wanted. I wasn't one of them, anyway.

He gently pried open my thighs to further his exploration. The first time he did this, I was self-conscious. As a curvy girl, I was never sure what men thought of my body. I didn't care when I was clothed, but once the clothes came off, all my self-conscious worries and anxieties moved in.

I always felt I had too much: hips, butt, thighs, and breasts. You name it, I had it- in overwhelming amounts, too. Yet, Carter never seemed to complain. He never hesitated. If he wanted to please me, he *did*. That was one reason why I loved him. But it was certainly not the only reason.

Hovering over my pussy, Carter teased the edges of it with his warm breath. He massaged my hips with his hands. "God, you're gorgeous. I never get tired of this view."

"Oh, Carter, you're driving me nuts. Truly." I leaned into him, shoving my pussy in front of his mouth to encourage him to move faster. He backed up and made a *tsk tsk* noise, his index finger waving in the air in front of me, issuing me a silent warning.

"Damn it, Carter. If you don't hurry up, I am going to get my jackrabbit out. It'll take care of me in no time."

He sat back on his heels and caught my gaze. Then he smirked. "No vibrator is as good as a man."

I lifted my eyebrows. "Oh? You know nothing, then."

"You can't tell me that a vibrator will do this." He moved swiftly, plunging his delicious tongue through my parted lips. I gasped. My back arched against the edge of the granite countertop, and I squealed. I grabbed at his short, black hair and cried out as his tongue thoroughly worked me.

His fingers started a dizzying dance, expertly strumming my entrance as if I were a guitar that longed to be played. I sensed the deluge flooding through me, watching it trail down his chin. He ignored its descent, wearing me like a badge of honor instead, while he continued licking his amazing tongue over my clit. Then, he delved lower.

My body vibrated. My legs trembled. My breath staggered. A rising sensation grew in my belly. I clutched his hair, holding on to it for dear life while silently urging him to continue. The urgency to scream rose up the back of my throat.

"Yes, yes, Carter, yes! Make me come. Make me come. Yes. Fuck." My head fell back with my pleas. I looked up at the ceiling, running my gaze across the knockdown texture while his sensual assault continued.

My eyes rolled to the back of my head. My body rocked in tandem with his. It was as if we had become one hell of an unbreakable pleasure ride.

My heavy pants for air grew out of control. I drew in quick, repeated, ragged breaths while he continued to tease me mercilessly, moving quicker, then slowing down, then moving faster once again. It was as if he was trying to draw out my pleasure. The cad.

Carter was incredible. He was the only lover who could do things to my body without even touching me. Just one sexy glance from him had me drooling like a sex-starved teenager. Yet, back then, Carter wasn't the same. He wore large, silver-framed, geeky glasses and had a haircut that looked like his mom had placed a bowl on his head and cut around the edges.

I dragged my gaze down to peer at him while he lavished his sole attention on the sweet spot between my legs. He wanted to please me so badly. He was doing a great job.

The Carter I knew today was amazing, and it wasn't all because of the sex. He spent hours in the gym carving his impeccable bronzed body into a work of art. I thoroughly enjoyed those moments. I was able to run my hands over his washboard abs, caressing my fingers over his tight ass and then continuing down his corded thighs. Afterward, I'd get on my knees and play the role of a willing, wanting prostitute. Carter always liked that. He'd watch me the entire time. I'd look into his eyes at the beginning, and then I'd open my mouth wide- as wide as I could- and seal my lips over the rim of his enormously long dick. Seriously. The man was hung. Yet, wasn't there a saying about black men? It was true. I knew why Carter had no problem getting dates. Next, I'd plunge down his rod as far as I could go, hoping to give him the best blow job of his life. *Every time*. Carter deserved my best. After all, he always gave me his.

Carter was bigger-way bigger than any of my past lovers, but then none of them were black. He was my first. In my heart, I hoped he was my last. Yet Carter had many women- most of them one-night stands. He wasn't up for long-term with anyone. This sad fact almost made me break my concentration, yet I whisked it away and gazed back at the face of my lover, working me in ways no other would have had the patience for.

I unglued the fingers of my right hand from his hair and caressed the side of his head. "You're so good, Carter. So good and so freaking bad, too."

His soft chuckle vibrated through me. It made me smile. I always liked making him laugh, even when it was at times like this. We had an easy friendship. One of mutual respect and collaboration. I never wanted this to end.

Still, there were times with him that I worried more than others. I was never sure how I compared to the women in his life—past and present. He hardly talked about any of them. Yet, he never complained about me, so I guess I wasn't that bad, unlike Eddie, who often complained about feeling my teeth on his dick. I tried hard not to do that, but I had a small mouth. It's not like I could take my teeth out to please him. The best I could do was try harder the next time, but somehow, it never seemed to satisfy Eddie. Carter, on the other hand, rewarded me with loud shouts and heavy panting afterward.

Carter did so much for me. He was always there for me. He deserved everything I had to give. He was that kind of *friend*.

He also willingly paid me back with times like this- delicious memories I held sacred in my heart. Wonderful dreams of him that stirred through my loins and tightened my pussy till it hurt. *God.* I wanted him inside me so bad. Yet, we never went there. We only teased on the surface. We never went all the way.

He called it *jacking each other off*. He heard the slang from one of his boys and thought it was perfect for our situation. I preferred a more romantic description like pleasing, teasing, and fucking without penetration. Any of the terms would do. They were much better at describing what we did than his callous terminology.

My back arched. I threw my head back and let my breaths fall in and out of me as I rocked harder, shoving my hips toward him, desperately seeking the pinnacle. I climbed the mountain, higher and higher, each level getting sweeter as I ascended. "Oh god. Oh god. You're so damn good. So damn, fucking good. Oh god, Carter. Oh god…"

He reached around me and spanked my left butt cheek hard. I cried out as the pain tingled and spread through my rear, the warm remnant of his handprint searing through my sensitive, fair-colored skin.

Replacing his tongue with his thumb, he continued to tease me, tipping backward to rest on his heels. He plunged his tongue into me, at the same time, caressing his thumb sensuously over and over across my sweet spot. "Come for me, Nya. Come for me," he said between penetrating thrusts of his delicious tongue. He watched me in between as he continued his sensual dance, strumming my guitar strings until my body was vibrating and singing. His glance swept over me as desire filled his irises.

I bucked as another wave of pleasure carried me away. Then I bucked again.

"Good girl. Come for me, Nya." He resumed his previous position. His luscious tongue gave me generous, long licks until something burst within me. I stilled. My head rolled back as I cried out to the heavens, shouting as my orgasm consumed me. He continued licking me, his tongue picking up speed, lapping up my juices.

I grabbed onto patches of his wavy, black hair as I wailed one more time. He snuck his hands under my buttocks when my knees buckled, lifted me back up, and steadied me with an uncommon ease. Then I doubled over, completely wiped out and supremely satisfied, while he eased to a stand, never letting me go. I tasted myself on him when he kissed me, his tongue probing through my parted lips. He held me tightly in his arms until my breathing regulated and my heartbeat slowed.

Carter smiled at me, caressing several fingers gently across my face as he regarded me with care and concern. "You okay? Was that too much for you?"

The bulge from between his thighs rubbed against my belly, reminding me that he hadn't had his turn. I licked my lips, pulled down his zipper slowly, and then pulled him out from his hiding place beneath his boxers. Then I surrounded his thick member with my hand and moved my fingers up and down, smiling with pride and wonderment as he grew bigger in my palm.

I sucked in the air when he slapped my hand away. "No. Tonight is your night. It's not about me. You're the one who caught your boyfriend cheating."

I whined. "But I want to please you, too."

Carter quickly tucked himself away and zipped up. He lifted me to a stand and then cupped my chin with his fingers, locking my gaze with his. I caught the glint of my love juices flowing over his chin. "No, baby girl. I want tonight to be all about you. Okay?"

I wrinkled my nose at him. "Okay, if you say so."

He leaned his forehead against mine. "Good girl. Now, can you stand on your own? I need to get a towel to clean up."

I gave him a lazy smile. "I'll just lean against the counter for support."

He pointed back at me as he walked away. "You do that. I'll be right back. I got your favorite for tonight, by the way. Jelly beans and popcorn. Go pick out a movie you want to watch. And yes…" He winked. "It can be one of your romantic movies. I don't mind. Not tonight. Tonight is *your* night. It's all about you, baby."

Damn. He was sexy when he called me baby. Too bad it wasn't true.

I called after him as he strode down the hallway toward the bathroom. "You are too sweet. You know that?" I swiveled toward the TV and then stopped in my tracks. "Wait a minute. Carter? Didn't you have a date, tonight? Carter?"

"I canceled it."

"You what? Why did you do that? You didn't have to do that. Seriously. You can still go out with her if you want. You don't have to stay here with me. I'm okay now."

He popped his head out of the bathroom and rubbed the white towel across his mouth several times. Still holding onto the piece of fabric, he replied. "I'd rather be with you unless you want to be alone?"

I shook my head. "No. I just wanted to give you the option in case you were really into her. I like spending time with you, Carter. I mean, you *are* my best friend."

He chuckled low. "Besides, you might need something later on. You never know. No man is ever worth your tears, baby girl- not when he cheats." He shook his head.

The corners of my mouth widened into a grin. "You are the best, you know that?"

He disappeared from the doorway. "Yeah, I know."

"Whatever. You egotistical maniac." I teased.

I heard his laughter seconds before he shut the door closed.

2

Nya

Carter was on a date, and I was stuck at home. Well, not really… I had my own car. I also had friends and places I enjoyed visiting, but I had no energy to do anything except sit on the couch, watch murder-mystery movies all day, and gorge on chocolate-raspberry ice cream.

Carter asked if I wanted him to stay back. I couldn't say yes. Not after the last two days of fun we had- alone- and at home. We spent our nights taking turns. I gave him blowjobs. He gave me trembles of immense pleasure up and down my spine as he took me to heaven and beyond.

We tried getting out of the house but, really, what was the point? Everything we had was right at home: the TV, food to eat, and several places, out of public view, to pleasure each other. Yet today was the third day. Even private companies requested a doctor's note after three days off in a row.

This morning, Carter sat at the edge of my bed—all six-foot-five glorious inches of him—to ask if I needed anything. I waved my hand in the air and dismissed him back to his job.

What I meant by that is—he went back to his room to sit at his computer desk to promote his dating app, Connex, all over social media. Not that Connex needed any more promotion. It was already a number-one hit among apps in the same category. Since Connex went viral, Carter had the luxury of working from home. I, on the other hand, worked from home, too, but remotely for a company I couldn't stand. Still, I had to stay with the company because jobs, in the current economy, were scarce, and there were bills to pay.

I offered to work for him, but Carter said that wasn't a good idea. Friendship and business didn't mix. Well- I had a different opinion. When I shared it with him-

"I think it could work out," I said.

"I don't."

Carter pulled up a website and click-clacked away on his keyboard while I continued arguing with him.

"But Carter, I don't think it's going to be a problem," I whined.

He waved his hand in the air in a stopping motion. "I do, and that's final."

I strode toward his desk and sat on the edge of it, shoving my face in front of him to get his attention with a flirty smile. "Well, I don't-" Before I could finish my sentence, he grabbed ahold of me and kissed me. Then he repositioned his hands and flung me over his shoulder, in a fireman's carry, like I weighed nothing. My legs kicked his stomach and then flung about, trying to find other parts of him to hit while I screamed. He started walking, our destination unknown to me.

He grabbed ahold of my legs, swung me around like a sack of potatoes, and then positioned me over something soft and firm at the same time. I found myself leaning over the back of the couch with my rear up in the air. It was a position I had been in before, but only when we were role-playing or playing, in general—never when he was upset.

Standing off to one side of me, he then proceeded to smack my bottom hard with the palm of his hand.

I squealed. "Carter," I said between gasps. "What are you doing?"

"Is this what you want, baby girl?" He said, in a commanding tone of voice that had my body warming, tingling, and perked at attention. "Is this what you want? Because I will give it to you. But you are *not* going to be my partner."

A tear formed in the corner of my eye. *Not his partner. No? Never?* He continued slapping my rear end, interspersing caresses and massages with more hard slaps to my bottom. I whimpered.

"Are you done now? Can I get back to work?" he asked.

A tear streamed down my face from the corner of my left eye. Carter must've seen it, for he swooped his right thumb out toward me and scooped up the water bobble onto his finger, holding it in front of his eyes for a few seconds, marveling at it before he crushed it between two fingers. He raised me to a stand and pulled me into his arms.

He patted my back affectionately. "Hey. I'm sorry. I didn't mean to make you cry."

I shook my head as I blubbered against his shirt, uncaring if my tears permanently stained the blue color. "No. It's not that. I like your playfulness."

He raised my chin up. "Hey, you okay, baby girl? Seriously. I would never harm you. You know that, right?"

I choked. "I know."

"Are you okay? Please tell me you are okay."

I nodded in response.

He pulled me into a tight embrace. "I am so sorry." I snuggled into his warmth, the heat of his body and his musky scent overwhelming me with a sense of peace. I smiled and nuzzled my head against his chest. Carter placed his head against mine and kissed my cheek. "I love you., you know."

"As a friend. Yeah. I know."

"*Best* friend."

My heart dropped into my stomach. Why did Carter have to remind me of our status all the time? I didn't want to remember.

A few minutes later, after making sure I was okay, he went back to whatever he had been doing before.

It was funny how Carter didn't want me to work for him, but he had tried to get me to use his dating app. It was hilarious, actually. Still, it seemed Connex worked for some singles. It certainly seemed to work for Carter.

Since Connex went live, Carter was never at a loss for dates. He was not only insanely wealthy but famous, too, now. I wondered why Carter stayed with me in the apartment when he could have bought a home in Beverly Hills if he wanted to. Yet, Carter hadn't changed much since Connex went viral. It was a fact I was proud of, for fame seemed to, sadly, change people, but Carter was still old, goofy, regular Carter- just more popular now.

He could have had any girl he wanted to, and he probably did since he mostly dated them, but strangely, he never seemed to settle on any *one* girl.

I caught him, one day, flipping through the pages of Connex, swiping right or left depending on his interest. I laughed when he placed his phone face down across his thigh as if I had caught him doing something he shouldn't be doing. This morning, he had tweaked his profile and found a new date- at least for tonight. He was out with Cindy right now, I imagined. I pondered what Cindy looked like according to what I knew of Carter's preferences.

I had to find out what he put on his profile. Thankfully, he showed me one day- the day he was trying to coerce me into paying for Connex.

"Look. You see how simple it is?"

"Yeah, I am not a wordsmith, Carter." I peeked over his shoulder and read part of his info before he scrolled down the page.

"Twenty-four-year-old African American male. Looking for someone to share experiences with. Same interests, a fun personality, and a good sense of humor. Are you the one I have been searching for?"

"Wait. I didn't get to read all of it," I protested as he swiped his profile out of view.

"You're not supposed to. Why don't you get on Connex yourself and then check it out? Just think, you might be able to find a man that is right for you."

I rolled my eyes as I walked away. I heard his soft chuckle behind me.

Glancing at my phone on the right side of me, on the comfy couch cushion I sat on, I picked it up, scanned the screen quickly, and then determined if there were any new messages awaiting me. After seeing nothing to pique my interest, I placed it face down by me, at the same time smoothing the tips of my fingers over the soft, patterned fabric of the couch. I had been fingering the material sporadically and at several times while watching the shows. I supposed it was a way to release my underlying anxiety plus try to gain comfort while sitting alone in the apartment while Carter was out doing God knows what with Cindy.

Noise suddenly flared up outside. The tone increased as the neighbors bustled by, slapping their shoes against the concrete. A boy screamed and then must've taken off running. Shoes clip-clopped quickly. The faint sound increased in decibel level and then faded past my front door indicating whoever it was, was heading toward an unknown destination. I turned up the volume on the TV, drowning out any remnants that lingered. The neighbors were always noisy, using the hallway as their playground. Sometimes, a ball would slam against our door. It was something one got used to living in the neighborhood we lived in.

Carter was used to it. He stated it felt like home. I, on the other hand, came from a more suburban lifestyle, and though I entertained the idea of moving to an "upper-class" neighborhood, I knew I wasn't going anywhere without Carter. Not until that fateful day, he met his queen, moved out, and married her- I shook my head to release the vivid image threatening my current state of peace. *Ohhh.* I didn't want to think about that. I crossed my arms over my stomach as a sudden nauseous sensation threatened to overwhelm me.

A second, sharper noise sounded. The tone changed to a familiar musical one that I recognized immediately. I picked up my phone and answered the call.

Carter's manly voice caressed my eardrums. "Hey. You want anything? Cindy and I are going to come over if that's okay with you."

"Um.." I glanced over at the empty bag of chips, the half-eaten pint of chocolate-brownie ice cream, and the open container of cookies on the ottoman in front of me and hesitated, unsure what to say next. Nestled comfortably in my soft fortress of solitude, I was not looking forward to company this evening. Yet, Carter did this all the time. He dated and bedded women the same day, constantly, while I, instead, took my time with a man before he saw more than the basic shape of my cleavage. Carter's style of dating couldn't have been more opposite of mine. He didn't believe in waiting, while I, as a single female, considered waiting to be the smart, cautious thing to do.

I gave my heart too easily. That was my problem. In these modern times, a woman had to be careful, for not everyone could be trusted, not like Carter. I had learned my lesson long ago. I wasn't going to jump into a relationship with someone I barely knew before a few dates were done. I had to know if there was something beyond basic attraction with any of my suitors. Carter begged to differ.

The only thing he cared about was a woman's looks. Oh, and the shape of her toes. It was so bizarre. There was nothing that would make Carter run away faster than jacked-up toes. That's how he put it. It made me laugh every time he said it. The nice thing was that he loved my toes. He thought they were cute and sexy, especially when my toenails were painted. He told me so many times.

The sound of my name brought me back to reality. I realized I hadn't answered Carter.

"Uh, I don't know. Maybe some chili cheese fries. Actually, that sounds pretty good. You know, comfort food and all." I stared at my fingernails and then turned my hand over to check out the palm of my hand.

"Comfort food? Are you okay? You want me to come home alone?"

Yes! I yearned to yell out the single word, rushing up the back of my throat and urging its release. Instead, I stifled it before I could utter it, unwilling to hurt Carter's feelings. There was no way I was telling Carter that. He would know something was up. I didn't want to alert him or hint at anything that could be wrong.

Besides, he was out on a date. He was entitled to have his fun. Just because I was home and in the dumps didn't mean everyone should join me. Although, it would feel a hell of a lot less lonely if I did my wallowing with others.

"No, I'll be fine once you bring the chili cheese fries home."

Goosebumps formed across my arms with his soft, husky laughter. *Damn.* The things he did to me, and he hadn't even touched me yet.

"Fine. I'll bring them home for you. See you soon." The call disconnected.

I lifted from the couch, raised my hands overhead, and stretched toward the ceiling with a loud yawn. Then I grabbed the empty bag of chips, crushing the bag in my hand to make it smaller. I wrapped the container of cookies and picked up my pint of ice cream and walked toward the kitchen. Throwing the bag of chips in the garbage, I opened a cabinet and shelved the cookies. Scooping the lid off the counter, I capped the ice cream container and then shoved it into the freezer, throwing the spoon into the empty kitchen sink, afterward. I'd rinse it off later and put it in the dishwasher when I cared. Right now, I wanted to mope and sink back into the sofa.

I rubbed my hind end into the couch, mushing sections of it to conform to my body like a comfortable memory foam bed. Then I flipped to my side and lay my head down on a fluffy pillow while my eyes glazed over, taking in random scenes across the TV.

A part of my heart throbbed painfully like it had been smashed into bits with a meat tenderizer. I wasn't unhappy yet I wasn't happy, either. I think I was somewhere in between, waiting for someone to pop out of nowhere and tell me it was all a rehearsal and none of it was real.

Breaking up with someone should have been easy. After seven months of my life that I will never get back, the bastard cheated on me. Still, a part of me didn't want to be mad at Eddie. I still loved him. The fool. Eddie and I had some great memories together. I thought he was *the one*. Apparently, I was wrong.

My heart and my mind seemed confused. They warred against each other. My mind still wanted Eddie to be a part of my life. Yet, my heart sought validation. Still- another part of me was ready to let go. *Knew* that Eddie wasn't that important to me anymore. Knew that I should move on. I was fine without Eddie. Yet, was it true?

A half hour or so later, an unusual sound caused me to stir in my sleep. I opened my eyes and turned my head toward the source to catch a woman's giddy laughter, accompanied by the sound of faint keys jangling in the background.

A whooshing sound ensued. The female's voice intensified as something slammed in the background. I peered over the back of the couch to find Carter's face suddenly looming over me.

"Oh!" I jerked back with a start as he stared directly at me.

He put his hands up in the air. "Hey. Sorry. Didn't mean to startle you. I saw you had the TV on, so I figured you were here. I just wanted to let you know that I was, too." A tall, slim, bubbly brunette walked up to him and smiled. He glanced toward her and then back at me before he made introductions. "Nya, this is Cindy. Cindy, Nya, my roommate."

We greeted each other. Cindy smiled wide, her perfect white teeth brimming beneath her painted red lips. I glanced over her, finding her thick, black hair in braids and her stunning ocean-blue eyes dancing with excitement. She had the perky body type I always wanted. The kind of body women worked hard in the gym to achieve but never seemed able to. Somehow, she had.

Cindy was beautiful. Sporting a slim waist, curvy bosom, and juicy derriere, she easily matched all of Carter's physical traits.

A sudden, painful sensation panged within my heart as I watched Cindy, but I chose to ignore it. I lifted my robed hand to shake hers as my gaze gave her the once over, again, not satisfied having viewed it and needing confirmation. Her painted red lips contrasted her pearly white skin, making Cindy look sexy yet sassy. Her silky red top flowed smoothly across her chest, accentuating her shapely bosom. The plaid, pleated mini made Cindy's shapely legs seem longer and even taller.

Cindy's outfit reminded me of a Halloween costume I spotted once. I had perused through costumes one year and found several schoolgirl outfits. This could have been one of them. All that was missing to complete the look was a long red tie, ponytails, and solid-colored glasses. Maybe she brought them with her. Maybe she had planned this all along- to woo and sucker my best friend, Carter, into a hot night of sex. Well- that's what Carter wanted anyway- from any of his dates. Cindy was just giving in to his wishes. I pondered what Carter thought of Cindy's outfit. Did he like that type of costume? Should I buy one to wear just for Carter? I could get back on my knees and play naughty school girl, begging for his lollipop. All I needed were knee highs to complete the outfit. Maybe black ones with a little lace around the top edges…

I shook my head to clear the rambling thoughts. *Whatever*… Regardless, Cindy looked hot, and I wasn't happy.

Cindy was looking fine and what was I wearing? *Hmmm.* I frowned as I glanced over my outfit. Well… I was, certainly, no competition for Cindy right now. I doubted my comical, raccoon-printed pajamas and my long, leopard print robe screamed sexy in any way, yet it spelled ultra comfort for me.

I glanced away from them in disgust. Did Carter have to pick tonight of all nights to drag home one of his women for a quick tousle in his bed? Couldn't they have gone to a hotel instead?

The urge to burrow into the soft cushions of the couch and let the night disappear into day tempted me to ignore basic social constructs and, instead, collapse back onto the couch while they headed to his bedroom.

Cindy grabbed ahold of Carter's hand, folding her smaller one into his. He pulled on her hand with a sexy grin and tugged her toward his bedroom. "Cindy put your chili cheese fries in the fridge. You might want to heat them up when you're ready to eat," he yelled over his shoulder as he led his next prey to the slaughter. He stopped in his tracks and turned toward me with a questioning look on his face. "Or do you want them now? I can heat them up for you if you like."

I stared at him for several seconds, unable to speak. He interrupted playtime with Cindy to ask me if I wanted food? That was sweet and so very *unlike* him.

I released Carter to return to his previous endeavors with a wave of my hand. "No, I'll be fine. You two have fun."

He winked before he escorted not-so-innocent Cindy toward his tawdry, beckoning lair. "Oh, we plan to." The he shut the door behind them while I caught a glimpse of Cindy wrapping her arms around his neck.

"Oh geez. Now I have to hear them going at it all night…" I mumbled under my breath, sinking lower into the cushioned walls of the couch.

I was right. I didn't have to wait long at all.

A loud noise banged against a wall, which I assumed was Carter's headboard. I had heard the same sound countless times before. The noise continued repetitively as I envisioned him having sex with her on top. She must've been holding onto the headboard for it to make so much noise. With her slim build and her over-the-top, surgically constructed bosoms, I could only imagine what Carter thought of her body. Did he prefer her skinny build over mine? I was nowhere near *slim*. I had too many curves and junk in the trunk, like no one's business. Carter seemed to like my rear, though, gladly grabbing onto it as he took me over the rainbow and back with that delicious, devilish tongue of his.

I heard a scream and then another. Cindy's excitable voice grew louder over the next few seconds. Choruses of "oh yes, oh yes," and "oh baby," hailed my friend, attesting to his grand, sexual prowess. I scooted from the couch, opened a drawer to the TV stand, and pulled out a set of Bluetooth headphones. Placing the pair over my ears, I cranked the volume up, shoved the drawer back in, and then flopped back onto the couch.

"Boy, I miss Eddie," I murmured under my breath as I snuggled into the sofa for the night. Sex with him was always fun and spontaneous. Well, mostly… I tossed out the image of him scolding me for raking my teeth across his dick.

With the commotion happening in Carter's bedroom at full throttle now, I knew it was going to be a very, very long night.

3

Carter

Cindy rubbed her hands across my bare chest before she kissed me goodbye. I enjoyed her lips one final time and then patted her bottom as she swished toward the door. Grabbing ahold of that ass last night was incredible—especially while I came—but it was nothing like grabbing ahold of Nya's ass while pleasing her... Cindy swiveled toward me, interrupting my thoughts. I looked up as she walked through the front door and gave me a backward wave.

Swaying her hips left to right, she sashayed down an imaginary runway, giving me the most delicious view of all that I had enjoyed last night *and* this morning. "Call me, lover," she almost begged.

Shutting the door behind me, I placed my back against it for several long seconds. I didn't respond to her comment on purpose. I never promised a woman anything—*ever*. One night was possible, but *two*? *Nah*. The lady would have to be extra special for me to consider a repeat.

It's happened before, though. I've had sex with women on multiple occasions over several days. Yet, it was rare. I could count on my hands the ones that held my interest long enough to go more than one day. That list included Nya.

I know—I know—I shouldn't be talking about my best friend, Nya, in that way. The fact that we're lovers surprises me to this day. I mean, Nya is a catch. Smart, capable, beautiful, and *way* out of my league.

Her fatal flaw? She dated losers like this last guy —*Eddie*. The fact that Eddie cheated on Nya—wow. Could the guy be any dumber? Why on Earth would you cheat on a gem of a woman like Nya?

I shook my head, not quite comprehending why she dated Eddie in the first place. She was just like that. Sweet and innocent in many ways but saucy and spicy in others. Anytime I recalled Nya's lips parting with happy sighs followed by heavy pants and then long, strong wails as she hit her peak, my groin immediately ached, and my cock stood rigid at attention.

Aching for the one thing we *didn't do*. Penetration. We have enjoyed and done many, many fun things. Still, we never did *that*. Nya liked to experiment, though. When Nya asks, I can't say no. I am up for anything as long as it involves Nya. Yet, abstaining from full-blown sex. It wasn't something we talked about. It was simply— *understood*.

The first time I grabbed her and rolled her back with me onto the bed to try something different, she gave me a long, warning stare that had my hands shooting straight up in the air. I wanted to go further with her, but she put on the brakes, citing my reputation with women. Could I help it that I liked women? Since Connex's popularity and fame, I had an endless list of willing and wanton females to choose from.

Nya didn't like my lifestyle. I wasn't ready to settle down. We stood at a standstill, neither willing to back down. It was from then that I knew sex was off the table, but everything else was negotiable.

We fondled each other in countless places: the shower, the movie theater, and even in my car. I had locked away the desire to have Nya mean more in my life a long time ago. This was all there was. Unwilling to lose Nya, I instead, accepted the terms of our relationship.

4

Carter

After several weeks of Nya moping around the house and going through the motions of a normal life, I sat her down and did something stupid.

"Hey. How have you been? I mean, how have you really been? You look lost or something."

She shook her head, opened her mouth twice, and then tried to convince me otherwise. "I've been good. Really, I have."

"No, you haven't. No, baby girl. I know you better than that. Come clean with me. Your heart is still hurting, isn't it?"

"So, what if it is? I mean, it's been a month. It hasn't been that long."

"Yes, it has. It's been a month. It's been way too long. The man was a loser, Nya. He didn't deserve you. He cheated on you. He was a complete loser. You need to get over him."

She rose to a stand. "Please stop saying that, Eddie."

I pointed at her. "What did you just call me?"

She slapped one hand over her mouth and made a noise. "Oh God, I just called you Eddie. I'm sorry."

I raised my eyebrows. "My point exactly. You've been dwelling on him too much. He's not worth your thoughts. You need a night out. Grab your stuff. Get changed if you want. We're going to a bar."

She put her hand out in a stopping motion. "What? No."

"You need this."

She waved her hand back and forth in front of my face. "But I-I'm-I'm not in the mood."

I tugged on her arm and gently dragged her over to her bedroom. "Exactly why you need it. I'm not taking no for an answer. You've been in the house for far too long. You need to get out of it and get some fresh air." I slammed the door behind her while she was in mid-protest. I shouted through the door. "And Nya…If you find someone at the bar, don't worry about me. I'll be fine." I smiled as she cursed aloud.

Twenty minutes later or so, Nya stood in front of me in a too-short mini and a flowing blouse whose V-cut shape overwhelmed my gritty, sleep-deprived eyes. I stared hard at the top of her perky breasts below the long neckline, rising then falling with her breaths before I tore my gaze away. I swallowed hard, closed my eyes, and blew out a long exhale, attempting to shove from my memory the erotic display she gave me.

Swiveling toward her, I opened my eyes and then locked my gaze on her large, incredibly gentle, brown irises. "Are you sure you want to wear that out?"

"Why not?"

Because you look like a damn hooker. I gritted my teeth, forcing down the urge to tell her exactly what I thought of the outfit that should only be worn around me. She was too innocent and too cute. Men could easily take advantage of her. Wearing something like that- I whistled low. I wouldn't be held responsible for what happened to the men who treated her wrongly because they thought they could get away with something they couldn't.

"You're very conservative in your style." I raked my gaze over her body, taking slow, longing glances at her naughty curves. "I'm not sure if you'll be comfortable in that and those heels are a bit higher than you like to wear. I saw you walk out here just now." I looked her in the eye, making a point of my last statement. The way she strode out from the bedroom, she looked more like a newlyborn giraffe just getting used to her legs rather than the smart, sophisticated female she was. Nya, apparently, didn't get my message.

She turned away and haughtily replied. "I'm fine." Staggering toward the front door, she held her hands out by her sides in an effort to keep her balance. Whether her intention was to keep her heels from turning inward or outward, I wasn't sure. Yet, I held back my natural inclination to laugh so I wouldn't hurt her feelings. My girl was definitely going to need someone to keep an eye on her tonight.

I placed my arm around the back of her waist, holding her steady, luxuriating in the feel of her standing next to me. Half escorting and half dragging her to my car, she slipped a few times before we finally made it.

"Baby girl, are you sure you're going to make it tonight? We don't have to go out if you don't want to. I'm serious."

She jerked her chin up. "I'm going to make it."

I smirked at her sassy defiance. I loved that about Nya. She wasn't one to give in to anyone. Yet, sometimes, she was stubborn. That part frustrated me. Still, it amused me, too, in some ways. Nya had a kind heart. She was a good, strong, capable female. She had qualities in her that not many other women had. I assumed that's why she became my best friend.

With some sort of renewed energy fueled by pure determination, Nya slipped from my grasp and trotted the rest of the way, successfully, toward the car. She stood by it, bending her knees in a rhythmic motion that had my mind dancing with her impatience. I slowed my pace to an almost sloth-like motion. I was messing with her. I knew it.

She waved her hand at me in the air. "Come on... Come on, Carter. Hurry up. You're going slow on purpose."

I was, but she didn't need to know that. I grinned at her. "This is my natural pace, baby girl. I can't help it if you're in a hurry." I worried about Nya. The way she was teetering, barely, on those heels…they were going to take her down at some point tonight.

"Do you do this to all of your girls?"

"My girls?" I snorted. *No. Just you when you're acting stubborn.*

Nya could get under my skin in ways no other woman ever could. What she wore tonight was all wrong for her. Not that Nya looked ugly. *Hell no.* The exact opposite was true. She looked incredibly hot. If I was her date tonight and she was not Nya but one of *my girls* instead, I'd have her, quickly, wrapped around my waist with those sexy heels on and not much else.

Those five-inch leopard print heels were doing something sensational to my cock. She never wore them before- not that I recalled. I wondered when Nya got them. I knew for a fact that I didn't have to look down at my pants. The way that my dick was eagerly yearning to be free and straining the front of my pants silently informed me it was already highlighting to the world in large, bold letters what I thought about Nya's sex kitten ensemble.

At the bar, Nya threw down several shots of something or the other. I had lost track of all she had consumed while she ran down the list of alcoholic beverages, trying each one with revelry and gusto as if they were appetizers on a menu.

"You need to slow down, baby girl." I cautioned. Placing my hand over her next glass, I eyed her in warning. She slipped her glass out from under me and brought it up to her soft, kissable lips.

My gaze riveted to her tongue as it darted out of her mouth and licked across her bottom lip. "I know what I'm doing."

She lowered her head back and swallowed. I watched as her throat worked its magic, making the colored solution in her glass disappear within seconds. My brain conjured up vivid images of her in another position, swallowing what I had to give instead.

I sighed, my eyes closing with the salacious image. Licking my lips, I glanced back at my Jezebel, my gaze grazing over the feminine curve of her supple neck. It climbed further up to her incredibly soft earlobe, tracing the outline of it hidden beneath long strands of her perfect hair. I reached for one small section and curled several more around my fingers, gently tugging at them while she lifted back up.

"What are you doing?" Her hooded eyelids folded over glassy eyes. The alcoholic adventure she undertook apparently having made an effect on her composure. Her hand reached for mine, covering the back of it fully and then quickly springing away as if she had just been bitten by a snake. I felt the instant zinging sensation as her fingers touched my skin. It was incredible and confusing at the same time.

Nya combed her fingers through the strands of hair I had twirled around my fingers, tugging them away from me and smoothing them out so they lay flat against her head. "You shouldn't do that. We're not at home or…on a date."

I tilted my head to one side and lifted one thick eyebrow. "Have we ever been on a date?"

"No."

Then why did you mention it? I left the thought lingering in the air, unspoken.

Suddenly, Nya dropped her head onto the counter, folding her face into the crook of one arm on the way down. She had too much to drink. She was likely drunk, sleepy, and hopefully not ready to throw up anytime soon. I hated puke in my car. It was nasty to smell and difficult to clean up.

I leaned closer to her so she could hear me over the loud music and the conversations surrounding us. "You need to throw up? You want me to walk you to the bathroom, or are you ready to go home?"

She uttered a rumbling sound as she rolled her head from side to side. "Ooh. This is really…soothing. Mmm…" Her murmurs grew louder as the motion of her head lulls continued. Then she jerked her head up. Her mouth dropped open, and then she laughed. She turned toward me. Her eyes were glazed over, her lids half closed. "Carter."

"What?"

"I think I'm really drunk. Can you take me home?" She ended her sentence in a sexy half grimace, half pout.

I smirked. "Yeah. Thank goodness I decided to be the designated driver." I lifted my glass in the air. "Club soda's been my friend all night."

"I'm your friend."

"Yeah, I know. That's why I'm taking you home." I threw several bills onto the bar top and hailed the bartender over. Then, I held my hand out to her to help her down from the bar stool. "Come on. Let's go."

5

Nya

Boy, what a night. I ended up suffering as a result of it, my head hanging over the rim of the toilet, puking my guts out throughout most of the daylight. I have no idea how I made it home without coloring Carter's interior. The motion of the car and the bumps in some of the roads we took had me gagging and Carter swearing at me. I hadn't been this drunk since—since, well—it had been a long while.

I had no idea what possessed me to down drink after drink. I think I was exploring the entire menu. I couldn't help replaying Cindy in my head, wondering if Carter was going to give her a call. Granted, it had been several weeks since their tryst, and there had been a few after

Cindy, yet she still stood out in my mind. Plus, the girls he brought home lately seemed to all fit the same theme: thin and over-sexed. I guess that's why I wore what I wore last night. I was attempting to get his attention. *Epic fail*.

If I was honest with myself, that's exactly what I was doing, too. Trying to mimic one of his whores, *ahem*..dates. I knew I was being callous, but I had a throbbing hangover that wouldn't go away, and I was not in a kind, giving mood.

Still, over the past few weeks, it seemed Carter had been slowing down on his pickups. In seven days, he would have bedded at least four women, yet last week, he only went out with one. It was a bit strange to me, and it had me thinking.

He even hung out less with his boys. The only time he seemed to get together with them was to play basketball or to hang out at one of their houses playing video games. He used to hang out with them a lot at the bars and now, he seemed to want to stay home more. I didn't understand why.

Carter… There was something about his touch back at the bar. That weird, magical spark shivered through me when I sensed Carter's hand. It sent a foreign but thrilling sensation straight through me. Yet, my brain was having trouble wrapping around why this single incident was different than all the others. It wasn't like we hadn't touched each other before. Why did I suddenly feel it now?

Throughout most of the next day, I kept replaying the moment our hands met and trying to figure out what had happened. Re-tracing each step, I watched his reaction and then mine as if I was pausing an imaginary remote control and fast-forwarding, screen by screen, through a movie to discover something important.

Did Carter feel it, too? If he did, he never mentioned it.

Worried for me, Carter stayed by my side throughout most of the night. He even waited to leave until I was asleep. He took off this morning only after I told him to go. I wasn't going to hold him back from one of the most important meetings of his life. He had an appointment with an investor. I recalled our conversation.

"It's a meeting I scheduled a while ago. I'm meeting with a person interested in buying Connex."

"What?" I jerked up in the bed and then regretted it. My right hand slapped against my forehead as intense pain shot through it. I slowly lowered myself back onto the bed. "Oh god, I shouldn't have done that."

Carter scooted a glass of water toward me. He pointed at a white pill on the end table beside me. "Here. Take an aspirin. It'll help you." I did as he advised. Then, I propped my head back onto the pillow between me and the headboard.

"If you need me here, I won't go."

I waved a hand dismissively in the air. "No. This is too important of a meeting. You just told me. Go to it. You gotta go. I just didn't know you were selling the app."

"Yeah. I've been thinking about it for a while now. I have other interests."

I massaged my fingers into my forehead. "Oh. Okay."

He tilted his head to one side. "You sure you are going to be, okay?"

"Yes, I will. Go, Carter, this is more important."

He regarded me for a long while in the silence. Then he sighed with resignation, kissed me on the forehead, and left.

I lay almost motionless in the bed as I pondered all that had happened back at the bar. I still couldn't explain the intense spark of connection we had last night. It was incredible and hard to forget. I had no idea why this one time of touching him seemed to stand out. Rolling off to one side of my bed to stand, I found my phone and dialed a number I hadn't called in almost seven months.

"Hello? Yeah. I need to call out today. Sorry. I'm not feeling well." I pressed the red button across my screen to end the call and then padded the rest of the way out the bedroom door and toward the kitchen, searching for the one magical potion that would bring me clarity and some semblance of joy. *Coffee.*

Popping in my K-cup flavor choice into the opening, I pulled down the lever and pressed the button to brew my heavenly beverage. I watched eagerly, in anticipation, as steam rushed out from the water reservoir, creating a halo of vaporization and temporarily clouding over part of the plastic bin.

Grabbing a ceramic cup, I placed it on the tray and pressed the second button to spew out the dark, liquid contents, adding my favorite Irish-flavored creamer and sugar substitute packets afterward. Stirring the delicious contents, I sauntered toward my comfy oversized chair while blowing air over the mug. Then I placed the mug onto a coaster on a side table and sat back into the cushions while my thoughts replayed the memory that had me perplexed.

It wasn't the spark that confused me. Carter was a good-looking guy. I always knew it. Yet, he was only my best friend. Once I touched his hand, there was an instant, automatic attraction I hadn't figured existed in all the years we've known each other. Something beyond ordinary friendship. Something that demanded much more.

The primal urge to pull him into my arms and keep him there forever consumed me. Instantly, my body craved his contact, marking and claiming him as my territory like some savage beast with a fresh kill.

I didn't care that there were others around. I just wanted *him*. I thought he wanted me, too.

I sighed, reminding myself, at the same time, of our relationship status and his perpetual bachelorhood.

Yet, I still wanted him. Not in my bed for one night or two. That I already had. I wanted more…

Picking up my phone, I pressed on the name that had been in my heart since yesterday. I waited as it connected and was eventually picked up.

"Hello." The deafening noise of cars honking and traffic rushing by greeted me in the silence.

"Carter. Are you done with your meeting? Can we talk?"

"Yeah. Are you okay?"

"How did it go?" I eagerly asked. My curiosity had to know the outcome.

His tone of voice lightened with his merriment. "Good. We signed a contract."

My jaw dropped in surprise. I glanced briefly at my phone's screen. "Oh wow. That's great news, Carter. I am so happy for you."

"Thanks, but Nya, you called me. Remember. We were talking about you. You okay?"

"Yeah. I just need to talk to you. Maybe later?"

"Sure. I have a few things to do, and I was going to come by later, but it'll have to be quick. I have a date tonight."

"Oh…" I clutched the phone, squeezing the protective casing between my fingertips as my voice trailed off. My lips slightly parted. My brain was numb. I had run out of things to say. Maybe yesterday meant nothing to him, after all. Maybe I should remain silent. No…I couldn't do that. Something within me wouldn't let me hold back any more secrets. I had to tell him how I felt, even if he didn't feel the same way.

"Nya? Nya? Are you still there?"

"Yeah, I'm here."

"Oh." He chuckled. "I thought you disappeared on me. Are you sure you're okay? I mean, you did drink a lot last night."

"Yeah, thanks for bringing me home."

He snorted. "Well, I wasn't going to leave you there."

"Yes, but still, I don't know what came over me." I lied. It was Cindy. That's what had come over me. Still, I was never fessing up to Carter about her. He didn't need to know. She was in the past, and now, he had a new date.

Carter chimed in. "Probably an urge for freedom. Who knows? I do the same thing, too, sometimes."

"Really? I never see it."

A brief silence ensued.

"You got your heart broken, Nya. I understand."

The raw, vivid image of Eddie leaning over a slim blonde with breasts that were too large for her frame popped into my brain. He murmured husky words at her while her breathy whispers begged for more. Then he nose-dived between her perky, uplifted peaks, his incredible tongue giving her all of the attention that should have gone to me. I slammed open the bedroom door, widening my view of them, and shouted his name. He jerked his head toward me. I will never forget the look on his face. Eddie's jovial, flirty grin was quickly replaced by fear.

After months of incredible freedom, I wanted, so badly, to erase all memories of Eddie. I needed to let go of him in order to move on with my life. Yet, somehow, Eddie had got to me. Maybe it was the loss. Maybe it was the betrayal. Maybe it was me thinking I was, somehow, not good enough to keep him…

"Nya, are you still there? I'm sorry I brought it up. I'm just letting you know that I understand. You know that I'm here for you. No matter what, baby girl."

The start of a smile curled the corners of my lips. I sniffled as I spoke, blinking back the fresh tears that surfaced with the nightmare memory.

"I know. Thank you. It's okay. I'm over him. He was a jerk." I lied a second time. Recalling how our relationship ended in my pain, I sensed the imaginary sharp daggers pivoting and carving deeper through the edges of my tender, healing heart. I trusted Eddie. I thought he was different. Yet, after what Eddie did to me…I knew that Eddie wasn't the one.

"Good for you. He was a jerk. You deserve much better."

"Yeah. I do." *I deserve you, Carter.* The sentiment lingered in the air, unspoken.

"I'll see you later, then. Around seven p.m.?" Carter offered.

"Yeah. See you then. Thanks." I disconnected the call. A shot of hope fluttered through my weary heart. Carter was coming home later. We would talk, and- Images of the two of us intertwined, smiling and deliriously happy, flooded my brain. Was it possible? After all this time, could we make it work?

We were already best friends. It was well known that friendship was the foundation of any successful, long-term, committed relationship. Yet, would Carter say yes to me? I was nothing like his typical dates. I was short, curvy, and heavy-set, yet Carter seemed to have no complaints about my body. Still, I couldn't help but feel out of place when it came to the usual choices he made regarding physical appearance.

We once had a conversation regarding our preferences. Tall, slim, buxom, and physically fit were his adjectives, none of which applied to me. Well… maybe the next-to-last one did.

And Carter? He easily hit all my categories. I recalled us laughing about that one. Carter even suggested that we date. I blew out the water I had been sipping on at the time, knowing that he was only teasing me. Yet now, the crushing realization of what I was about to do had me partially frozen in fear.

What if he didn't accept me? It would all come crashing down.

If that happened, I wasn't sure what I would do. I couldn't imagine life without my best friend in it. Yet, the idea of him rejecting me... I took a step back and leaned forward over my legs, my hands gripping firmly onto my thighs for support as a numbing pain suddenly seared through my gut. My breaths see-sawed in and out for several long seconds as my heart stuttered. Life without Carter? Impossible.

Regardless of what he thought about me, I had to tell him. He deserved to know the truth. Even if it changed the nature of our relationship-in a negative way.

I rose to a stand and squared my shoulders back as I inhaled a long, calming breath of air. I held my head high, ready to face him with whatever outcome happened. If he didn't accept me, life would go on. I might have to take a brief vacation away from him to settle my thoughts and consider my next step, but I wouldn't let possible rejection stop what I had to do. I couldn't negate my feelings any longer. If that meant I had to step out of his life afterward, I would. Still, Carter would know the truth.

6

Carter

Mina clasped my hand in hers and giggled with girlish delight.

Holding my index finger up to my lips, I cautioned her with a *shhh*. "I have to talk to my roommate before we go out. Give me a minute, will you? I'll be out as soon as I can."

Mina released my hand. She smiled and rubbed her hands together. "Ooh. I feel so dirty."

I winked. "You are. You'll be even dirtier after I get through with you."

Her grin widened. A twinkle spread through her brown irises. "You're so naughty. How come we haven't met before?"

Because I didn't know you before this afternoon. I let the thought linger in my head.

Voluptuous and tall, Mina was a hot-headed Hispanic with long, flaming red hair, which was obviously unnatural but colored to a radiant perfection. She had generous curves that I couldn't wait to grab ahold of while I plowed into her from behind. It was the most vivid image I had intruding into my head of what I wanted to do with her. Next, she would be straddling my lap, gloriously and deliciously nude, while I plunged into her full force. Mina was up for everything I had to give, and after last night with Nya, I had quite a lot to work out.

My thoughts flitted to Nya. When her hand sprung from mine yesterday, I could've sworn she felt the same thing I did. I watched her carefully after that. She was drunk, and it was unclear if she felt anything at all after her initial reaction. Regardless, I did.

The recollection has lingered in my mind ever since. I washed off the memory later that night in the shower. Images of Nya floated across my mind while I bellowed out her name. Glorious spurts of cum painted abstract art across my shower walls in her honor. Sighing out her name later, I resumed the reality of our friendship as I made it back to my bed. It wasn't the first time I had thought of Nya as more than just friends, and it likely wouldn't be the last.

Tonight, I was going to enjoy a willing, warm body instead of my cold hand. I couldn't wait to wrap Mina's long, sensuous legs around my waist.

I placed my index finger across my lips and reminded Mina to be quiet. She waited in the hallway while I entered the door to the apartment. Closing it behind me, I shouted for Nya.

"I'm home," I called out, checking my immediate area but not finding her. My gaze swept toward her door, which remained closed.

A muffled voice beckoned from the other side. "Be right there."

I shifted over to the sofa and rested my arms across the back of it. I had just nestled my back and rear end into the cushions when she hastily exited her bedroom and stepped into my view.

"Hi," she grinned, slipping beside me. My right eyebrow lifted as I scanned over her. Instead of her usual oversized pajamas, she wore a silk robe. What lay beneath remained hidden from my immediate view. As if noticing my confusion with her choice of garment, she widened her grin and grabbed onto my left arm, sliding her small hands around it and holding it tight.

"I'm so glad you came home so we could chat."

Consciously aware of Mina waiting outside the door, I leaped into the conversation, hoping this wouldn't take too long. "So, what do you want to talk about?"

"Us."

I eyed her curiously. "What about us? We're good."

She enthusiastically nodded her head. "Yes, I know. That's exactly what I want to talk to you about."

I shook my head. "You're confusing me."

Her eyes widened slightly, and her voice softened to an almost whine. "Don't you want more?"

"Huh?"

"Didn't you feel it? Yesterday? I felt it. I thought you did."

My brain scanned through random images of yesterday. Did she mean? Was she talking about? *Nah.* It couldn't be what I was thinking.

She dropped her hands and stood up. "The electricity between us. The intense attraction."

My jaw dropped as the realization that Nya felt what I had hit me. She wanted to talk about it now. Yet, Mina was waiting for me on the other side of the door. I sighed heavily. The timing couldn't be more wrong. "Oh, Nya."

"I mean—I *felt* it." She loosened the ties to her solid lavender-colored silk robe. The smooth material dropped to the floor at the same time as my jaw. An instant zinging sensation hit my groin as I gazed at her, my eyes roving over every scandalous curve exposed by her flimsy, leopard print teddy. My gaze shot straight toward the deep V, barely hiding her beautiful breasts.

Nya. My naughty, delightful Nya. I entertained each sensual bump of her female form as my eyes lowered. Her sincere tone of voice zipped me back to reality.

She threw her hands out to her sides. "Do you want this or not?"

Are you kidding me? Hell, yes, I want you. I kept the thought to myself, my body responding with my desire instead. Nya was nuts if she thought I didn't want her. I shifted in my seat, trying to cover up the ever-increasing bulge tenting the front of my pants. It was, likely a pointless maneuver as her gaze had already dropped to that area and swept over it several times.

My head jerked toward the door as it abruptly swished open. "Lover, what's taking so long?" I spotted Mina widening her stance and placing her hands on her hips. She glanced over at me, first, then at Nya, and then back at me. She narrowed her eyes and looked at me. "What in the hell is going on here?"

Nya swung in her direction, giving me a gorgeous view of her black-lace thong squeezed tightly between two plump, round butt cheeks. My eyebrows shot up seconds before I scrambled to my feet, at the same time, sweeping up from the sofa the forgotten robe and shoving it toward Nya to cover herself. She pulled the flimsy material over her top, not bothering to cover her luscious ass, before swiveling toward me. Her flirty smile was long gone and replaced with a scowl.

"You brought a woman home?" Instead of waiting for my response, she rushed toward her bedroom.

"Nya! Nya!" I shouted after her. She slipped behind her door and slammed it closed.

Mina stalked toward me. Her caramel brown irises filled with rage. She jabbed one long, manicured nail into my chest. "You know what? I'm not into this bullshit. If you wanted a threesome, you should've asked me first. I'm outta here."

I called after her. "No. It's not what you think."

Mina didn't stop. Instead, she left, slamming the door behind her so hard the walls shook with the reverberation, and I worried for the few paintings of Nya's that still hung on the wall. Luckily, they held on for dear life until the shockwave settled.

What a wonderful night, I thought ruefully. I had pissed off two women, but there was only one whose opinion of me I was truly concerned about. I turned toward Nya's closed bedroom door. "Nya." Calling out her name, I quickly strode toward her door. I tried the doorknob and found it locked. I pounded on the thin slab of wood and shouted louder. "Nya! Come out of there, please. We need to talk."

"Oh? Now you want to talk to me? I thought you had a woman for that. Didn't you bring one home with you for-for—oh, never mind. You never want to talk to *those* women, anyway. You just want to screw them."

"Nya! That's not fair. I didn't know you wanted special treatment tonight. You should've told me on the phone. Come on out of there. This is not right. I thought we were just going to talk."

"You still don't get it, do you?"

"Nya, please. I hate talking to doors. I want to talk to you."

Sarcasm rippled through her voice. "Oh, *now* you do?"

I lowered my shoulders. "Nya. I'm sorry. Please come out here and face me."

The door creaked. I threw it open and rushed through it before she changed her mind. Grabbing at her shoulders, I shoved her gently toward the nearest wall and blocked her escape with my body, holding her still until her shoulders sagged and she finally gave in. We stared at each other for long seconds, trying to search for something in the other.

Nya was so beautiful—even now, as she attempted to figure out what I thought—I couldn't stay mad at her for long. I lovingly caressed the side of her cheek with the back of my hand and sighed. "Talk to me, baby girl. What did you mean by what you said before?"

"Where is that woman?"

"Mina? She's gone. It's just you and me now. No one else." My fingers caressed the edges of her robe, the smooth material to her right side threatening to fall off her shapely shoulder.

"That's how it should be."

I leaned closer, purposely letting my warm breath caress across the sensitive juncture where her shoulder and neck met. I knew she liked it. I knew this affected her.

She rolled her eyes and uttered a short squeal. I planted a lingering kiss to silence any further protest on her part.

"Nya, you're talking in riddles. Tell me what you want."

"I want you, Carter. I think I've always wanted you. I've been waiting for you to notice me as more than your best friend."

I slipped my hand behind her neck, supporting it and tilting it up so she gazed straight into my eyes as I ran my fingers through long strands of her hair. "How can this be? My best friend." Blazing a trail of kisses up her neck and over her chin, I nibbled my way back down. My voice turned husky. "Nya…Why have you never mentioned this to me before? How long have you felt this way, baby girl?"

"I just realized it yesterday when we touched." She lowered her head and sighed. "Maybe I was the only one who felt it, but I thought you felt it, too." She attempted to slide out of my grip, but my hands grabbed at her arms, holding her tightly to me.

"No. I felt it, too. I just wasn't sure if you felt the same way. I haven't been able to think of much else since yesterday. When I met Mina tonight, I thought a night out with a beautiful woman would take my mind off of you. I was foolish. I was weak. I should've come back to you and talked to you about it. I should've let you know my feelings and worked it out with you before I sought another. I'm sorry, Nya. Can you forgive me?" I tilted her chin up to find her slight smile. Then I swiped at a few stray tears streaming from her eyes. "Don't cry, baby girl."

"Oh, Carter. I love you. I don't want there to be anyone else anymore."

I shook my head. "I don't want that, either. Are you sure about this, though? It will change *everything*."

She snorted. "It already has."

7

Carter

I lowered my lips to hers and slipped my hands beneath her half-open robe, letting my fingers explore every familiar curve. My hands glided over her soft skin as her lips parted. I swept my tongue through her wet cavern, uttering a guttural groan as our tongues tangled together. I pulled at the lace of her teddy, impatient to get to the prize awaiting beneath it. She shoved my hand away and made a *tsk-tsk* sound. Her flirty grin had my groin lengthening and standing at attention.

Reaching for my hand, she pulled me toward the bed, urging me to undress. I stood beside her, my fingers grabbing at her teddy and her bra and removing them quickly. I heard her chuckling in the background as my movements became faster, and my craving for her bordered on voracious. I lunged at her, placing my weight on my hands beside her head and my knees between her lovely, parted thighs.

She placed her hand against my chest and stopped me. The serious look in her eye gave me pause. "No more women, Carter."

I shook my head. "No more, Nya." I tilted to my left and placed my right hand over my heart. "I love you, Nya." Then, I eased forward. "I'm going to show you tonight how much, baby girl." I smiled at her. "It'll be our first time together."

"Yes, I know. And I love you too, Carter. I'm excited and scared at the same time, but I am willing to do this—*with you*."

I lowered my forehead, resting it gently on hers. "There is nothing we can't get through together. I would never let you fall. Never, Nya. I love you too much. I'll catch you. Every. Single. Time."

Her breathy whisper caressed my eardrums. "I know you will, Carter."

I lowered myself. Aiming for the sensitive juncture between her neck and shoulders, I planted a winding, erotic trail of torrid kisses, ending somewhere between her thighs. She grinned as I tugged at her black thong, urging her to dispense with the offensive object. Soon after she discarded it, I lowered myself down her luscious body, kissing my way to the spot, now only reserved for me. I slipped my tongue out, sliding it easily between her folds and grinning with pure male pride at her pleasurable scream.

Tonight was going to be a long night of pure ecstasy. A nice, long one. I was going to make sure of it.

But first…

I winked as I grabbed ahold of her hand. "Let's go take a shower."

She wriggled out of my grip with a protest. "But I already took one."

"Not the one I have in mind." I tugged at her, at first, and then positioned myself beside her, leading her toward the master bathroom. Our place had two bedrooms and two bathrooms. Nya had her own bathroom, except mine, the master bathroom, was much larger. It had enough room for the both of us, especially for what I had in mind for tonight.

We shucked clothing as fast as we could and then stepped into the shower stall that was big enough for a family of four. I slid the clear glass door closed behind me and stared at her. I had seen Nya naked several times before, but I don't think I ever really *saw* her naked.

I moved toward her, letting my fingers do the walking, strumming her sides and roaming my hands all over her, making sure I caressed her mounds, flicking her nipples to her moans, and then settling my fingers between her thighs.

"My God, Nya. You are so gorgeous."

She laughed. "You've seen me countless times, Carter."

I shook my head. "No. Never like this. Before, you weren't mine, but now Nya." I gazed into her eyes. "You are mine now." I smiled, pride swelling through all the previously empty crevices of my heart.

I touched every part of her delicious body, my fingers roaming freely across every curve as I followed each with a kiss, worshiping the queen before me. I lowered to my knees as my kisses trailed toward the path that demanded my attention. My fingers delved gently between her thighs as I delighted in her slight gasps and sounds she made. I followed my fingers across her clit with my tongue, folding my tongue easily and completely through her folds, starting my adoration of the goddess she was, slowly at first and then demanding more from her with every second.

"Oh, Carter." She grabbed ahold of my hair, her short nails digging into the skin. I didn't mind it. It didn't hurt much, and it showed me that she liked what I was doing to her. I wanted to do so much more. To take her to the highest depths as she did, every time, with me.

As I strummed my tongue across her, concentrating my full effort on the sensitive spot that would give her the most pleasure, I sensed myself growing larger, the tip demanding her mouth. I pictured her on her knees, her mouth covering the tip of me, and then soon regretted it as desire and want washed over me.

"Oh, Carter. Oh God. I am going to come."

Yes. She needed to, for I would soon be there with her if I didn't stop soon. Nya was so sexy. She had such power over me, and she didn't know it. I was never going to tell her, either.

"Oh god, yes!" She threw her head back and screamed, her fingernails digging further into my skull as her orgasm crashed through her. Her legs shook, and her knees vibrated. I held up her sexy bottom in my hands and continued pleasuring her, lengthening her enjoyment until she shoved my forehead from beneath her with a loud gasp.

I gave her a wide smile as I stood and kissed her fully on the lips, slipping my tongue within her wet cavern so she could taste herself.

We leaned our foreheads together as her breathing slowed and returned to normal.

"God, Carter. You are so damn good."

I chuckled.

"Now it's your turn."

"No." I grabbed ahold of her arms as she started lowering to the floor. "I can't wait that long. I need you now."

She shrieked as I swiveled her around to face the wall.

"Place your hands against the wall. I can't promise I will be slow."

"Oh, Carter. Take me the way you want to, baby."

Something in me snapped. My dick was thoroughly pleased with her statement. I slipped my fingers toward her pussy and fingered the entrance. She was so wet. So damn wet for me. It was a sin to have someone this eager and wanting, but here she was- my Nya- staring over her shoulder at me with an innocent, girlish eagerness I had never seen on another woman. She was so damn sexy, and she was going to get all of me.

I grabbed ahold of her hips and lowered my mouth to whisper in her ear. "I love you, Nya. You are my queen, baby girl. My queen." Then, I positioned myself and slowly entered her once-forbidden domain.

She gasped as I monitored her reaction. As sexy as Nya was, she had never been with a black man before. I knew that and was consciously aware of it, even with my dick telling me it wanted Nya-and now. I slowed myself to allow her to adapt to me because I wasn't your average size.

Almost as if in confirmation, she lowered her head and muttered. "Oh my god, Carter, you are so huge." I couldn't help my wide smile behind her. My heart filled to capacity with pride.

"Do you like it, Nya? Am I hurting you in any way?"

"Oh no. I like it. You feel so good. Keep going."

I chuckled and then took it a step further, slipping faster inside of her till she took almost all of me. Then I seasawed inside her to her moans and murmurs while I uttered a guttural groan. Nya felt so good. So perfect. Her pussy was damn perfect, like it was meant for only me.

I moved faster, plunging into her and then out in a dizzying rhythm that had us both gasping for air.

"Carter, Carter, oh god." My Nya was plastered to the wall, her energy depleted, her body moving in rhythm across the smooth tile in response to my rocking motion.

Pleasure zipped through me, ebbing and flowing through my body, increasing in intensity with every second of friction. I caressed her sides, whispering dirty things to her.

"My queen. My sexy ass queen." I smacked her bottom to her low squeal. "You are mine now, baby girl. All mine. All mine. You hear me, you dirty girl. I love you. You're all mine."

I held her still as I hit the peak of the mountain. Throwing my head back, I shouted, tipping over the edge. "Fuuuck, Nya…!"

I collapsed, leaning my body over hers, waiting for my breath to regulate and my rapid heartbeat to return to normal. I folded her into my arms, pulling her back into my chest, my head resting against her right shoulder and then

I smiled. Nya was mine. She was finally mine. Damn, that was incredible. I never would have considered it a possibility.

A mixture of gratitude and pride swirled through my heart, knowing that my brave girl took the first step and told me she wanted me for more than a friend. If that had never happened, we would not have had the best mind-blowing sex I had ever experienced.

I should have acted first… Yet, I didn't think it was possible. Nya was my best friend. We had great fun together. She made me laugh and was at my side with every downfall in my life. She meant everything to me. I never figured she wanted me- in that way. Man, was I wrong.

Regret rushed through me. I wasted so much time on other women when we could've been together.

"I'm so sorry, baby girl." I turned her effortlessly in my arms to look up at me. I swept a stray strand of hair out of her face and gazed into her eyes. "I am so sorry I didn't recognize what you meant to me. You have always been much more to me than a friend. I love you, Nya. I'm so glad you spoke up tonight. I was about to make another stupid mistake. You stopped me, my beautiful queen." I nuzzled her cheek and then her neck. Our lips met, and I gave her the sweetest kiss of enduring gratitude.

She chuckled.

I eyed her. "What?"

"I love you so much, Carter. I've wanted you forever."

I gently leaned her back into the spray of water pouring down from the showerhead, my hands skimming down her back and over her luscious backside. I swirled my fingers in endless circles across the smooth, plump skin, interspersing soft massages as I enjoyed her juicy globes. Nya's generous curves always got me going in ways that gave me thrilling yet unfulfilled morning glories.

"I am a fool, Nya. I have wanted you for so long since the day we first met. You don't know how many nights I have spent frustrated and thinking about us in this way. I wanted you so bad, baby. So very bad. Feel what you do to me." I covered her hand in mine and lowered it onto me, delighting in her slight gasp as she felt my excitement.

She brought her hands to my chest, leaned her chin against them, and gave me a sultry smile. "Oh, Carter. Don't you know? Those days are over with, babe. You don't need to think of me anymore. I am yours now, anytime you want, especially after the way you just made love to me." She glanced down at my dick. "Oh yeah, babe. You are so big, and I love it." She winked. "I really do."

I pivoted us ninety degrees so that my back end was now under the rush of water instead of hers. Gently shoving her back against the tile wall, I ordered her to wrap her arms around my neck and hold on tight seconds before I lifted both of her legs off the floor. Positioning her thighs across mine, she interlaced her feet behind my back, somehow knowing exactly what I wanted.

"Well then, baby girl. You better get ready for me because our first time will definitely not be your last. We are going to have a long, long, fun night together." She squealed with anticipation and gave me a wide smile I had to kiss.

As my lips met hers, I thrusted into her, taking care to let her adjust to my size. She made a satisfying sound seconds before I sealed our fates with the most passionate kiss.

Nya was mine. I was never letting her go.

Epilogue

I stepped across the tile floor of our newly purchased three-bedroom, two-bath house. Crossing into the kitchen, I threw my arms around Nya and leaned my head to rest across her left shoulder.

"Good morning, my Queen. Did you sleep okay?"

Nya sliced into a bell pepper, setting the majority of it aside to concentrate on dicing the portion in front of her. "Yes, I did, and you?" She swiveled toward me, dropping the knife back onto the cutting board while I half groped, half pulled her into my arms.

Our lips met and I gave her a passionate kiss seconds before I trailed a burning path of kisses down the side of her throat toward her shoulder. Lowering to my knees, I reached for her belly and caressed it, imagining feeling through the soft cotton of her nightgown one of the best gifts she ever gave me.

Then I placed kisses upon her belly as I whispered my new son's name. *Jabari.*

She lightly slapped my left hand. "You better stop. We don't know if it's a boy or a girl."

"I'm hoping for a boy."

"I know."

"But you know I will love any child of ours because it came from you and me, baby."

Nya smiled. "I know. You're going to be a great dad."

"I hope so. I know I will do my best."

"I know you will." I returned to a stand and nibbled across her shoulder. "Oh, Carter, you keep that up, and I am going to have the baby right here."

I laughed as I continued nibbling across her luscious, creamy skin. "I can't stop. I won't ever. So, you better have the baby right here, then."

Nya laughed, her belly shaking with her movements. Then she gasped aloud as a clear, filmy liquid seeped from beneath her nightgown and splashed across the tile floor. We looked at each other, and our eyes widened with alarm.

"Oh no. I think the baby is coming."

I shook sense back into my brain and sprang into action. "I've got you, baby. Let me get my keys. You just go by the door."

"But wait. I am in my nightgown."

Sprinting into the bedroom, I grabbed her robe, threw some pants on, grabbed my keys and wallet, and ran back toward her. I helped her into the robe and swung open the door, letting it close behind us as I led Nya toward the car.

Helping her into the car, I then ran around to the driver's side, slammed the door shut, and pushed the button, listening as the car came to life.

"I didn't expect the baby this soon," Nya exclaimed.

"It's okay. *He* will let us know when he is ready to be born."

She made a cute pout. "*She*. It could be a she."

I chuckled and shifted the car into gear, aiming the car toward the highway.

It's funny how life circumstances sometimes change everything. I once thought meeting Nya had made my life complete. I was about to be shown how wrong I was.

Did you like Romancing the Roommate? Check out the first Chapter of another one of T.K. Lawyer's steamy contemporary romances, Picture Im-perfect, available now!

1

What in the world had she gotten herself into?

Natalie's book was ready. Yet, her cover artist was in the hospital... In the past week, she had tried reaching out to several others with the experience and the skills needed to help her. But all declined, stating they had deadlines to take care of and that it would be months before they would even get to her project.

She had already announced the upcoming release of her book. Her heartbeat quickened as she considered the possibility of not following through with her promise. She couldn't do that to her readers.

Natalie's heartbeat sped to full gallop as panic set in. She swiped the back of her hand across the sweat beading across her forehead. This had never happened to her before. She had never missed a deadline. If she didn't have a cover- The possibility stilled her heart and rendered her mute. What was she going to do? Her fans had waited for too long for her next release with heady anticipation. She wouldn't let them down.

Ideas zipped through Natalie's mind, firing in rapid succession as she zipped through each possibility, swiping it left and out of her mind as if on a dating site searching for her perfect match.

Natalie's eyes widened as a possible solution floated above her head like a light bulb in one of those old cartoons.

"Wait a minute." She snatched her phone off the table next to her, unlocked it with her passcode, and then clicked on one of the multitudes of icons across her screen. She then clicked on an arrow at the top right of the page, which took her off the popular social media site and into a private messaging program.

Biting into her bottom lip, Natalie scrolled slowly through the multitude of names, eyeballing the miniature pictures next to each and searching for the one she wanted to contact. If she could find her, she might be able to help. She scrolled halfway down when she huffed out a long, deliberate sigh. Then she scrolled back up again just in case she missed her name. Scrunching her eyebrows together, Natalie reversed direction to discover the rest of the names on her list in the hopes she hadn't come across her yet.

She grunted in frustration. "Where is she? I know she's here. I've contacted her before, but it's been a long time. Oh please... she has to be here. Am I missing her name, somehow?"

Her thumb stopped its downward slide as she sucked in a breath of air. *Martina Jacobs.* She stared at the familiar name, but the picture beside it was not hers. It was a man, a very handsome man. He was an incredible Adonis with a broad chest and impeccable abs. Was it Martina, or did someone steal her account?

Cautionary words lingered in her mind, warning Natalie to tread carefully, but she had no chance to play devil's advocate. Not now. She was desperate. She needed help. She would have to throw caution to the wind, hoping that what she was about to do was what she intended.

The last thing she wanted was to contact Martina and find out it was some weirdo, instead posing as her and wanting money or worse, from Natalie. If they started asking Natalie for her bank information, she'd know immediately something was wrong. She would end the conversation as quickly as she started it and block the person from contacting her ever again. She crossed her fingers and then clicked on Martina's name and started typing.

Hey. Been a long time. Hope you're doing well. Can I talk to you about your models? I need a cover. Let me know. Thanks.

The response came back quicker than she expected.

Tell me what you're looking for on the cover. What genre? What does the main character look like?

Natalie tapped her index finger across her chin. Hmmm... She had vied with several competing images this past week, narrowing down what was essential and what mirrored the book's main contents.

After a few long seconds, her fingers hovered over the keyboard and then flew across it feverishly.

Contemporary Romance. Well... my main character is self-assured, wealthy, a bit of an entrepreneur, and into keeping healthy. He has to be good-looking, with dark brown hair and brown eyes. About five feet, eight inches or taller with a nice build, firm chest, you know, the drill. Like my past covers.

Natalie had been drooling over the lust-filled images popping up randomly in her head for the past week. All in anticipation of the sexy, hard-bodied men her cover artist would come up with. Then she received the shocking news about her cover artist. Natalie's stress level went from nil to the danger zone in one second as she scrambled for a backup plan.

Do you want the guy in a certain pose? By himself or with someone else? Want something in the background?

Did she want him in a pose? Natalie chuckled, her smile serious as she considered what she expected her cover to look like. Natalie stared at the screen, ready to respond, when Martina's next text message popped up.

I think I have the right guy. He's kind of new, though. Hasn't been on a cover yet, but he fits your description to a tee. What do you think? I can send over some images for you to look at.

She licked her lips while her fingers tapped across the keyboard.

Sure. I want him by himself, maybe inside a building with windows in the background and a skyline?

Cool. I'll send you a few images of him you can look at. If he works, I'll send you the contract and work on some mock-ups for you.

That's wonderful. Thanks.

Natalie blew out a happy sigh of relief. After a week of hopelessness, this conversation placed a ray of sunshine back in Natalie's path. In the past, Natalie had perused images of Martina's models, curious about their appearance. Although she did not know the particular one Martina referred to, she was sure any of them would do. They were all sexy, inspiring, bold, ripped men. She was able to picture any of them on her book covers.

International Bestselling Author, Tamara K. Lawyer, writes under the pseudonym T.K. Lawyer and was born in Colon, Panama. She moved to the United States with her family to pursue her post-secondary education aspirations and found her love of writing shortly after.

She writes sexy, heartwarming, paranormal, and contemporary romances. Her books often toe the line, straying from traditional ideas to open readers' minds and hearts to unlimited possibilities.

When she isn't reading or writing, she is likely spending time with her husband/best friend or catering to their lovable American Foxhound, Misfit, who steals all the attention in their house.

Connect with T.K.
Newsletter

Also, By T.K. Lawyer

(The Guardian League)

Stand-Alone Novels

Milton Keynes UK
Ingram Content Group UK Ltd.
UKHW030852040824
446426UK00001B/7